You and Me and
MISERY

Rayel Louis-Charles

An imprint of Enslow Publishing

WEST **44** BOOKS™

Please visit our website, www.west44books.com.
For a free color catalog of all our high-quality books,
call toll free 1-800-542-2595 or fax 1-877-542-2596.

Cataloging-in-Publication Data

Names: Louis-Charles, Rayel.
Title: You and me and misery / Rayel Louis-Charles.
Description: New York : West 44, 2020. | Series: West 44 YA verse
Identifiers: ISBN 9781538382776 (pbk.) | ISBN 9781538382783
  (library bound) | ISBN 9781538383391 (ebook)
Subjects: LCSH: Children's poetry, American. | Children's poetry,
  English. | English poetry.
Classification: LCC PS586.3 L658 2020 | DDC 811'.60809282--dc23

First Edition
Published in 2020 by
Enslow Publishing LLC
101 West 23rd Street, Suite #240
New York, NY 10011

Copyright © 2020 Enslow Publishing LLC

Editor: Caitie McAneney
Designer: Rachel Rising

Photo Credits: Cover cifotart/Shutterstock.com.

Printed in the United States of America

CPSIA compliance information: Batch #CS18W44: For further information contact
Enslow Publishing LLC, New York, New York at 1-800-542-2595.

I Think...

I'm falling in love. But, how can I be sure about her if I'm not even sure about myself?

I Hate Myself

but I read that
if you hate something
that means you still care. And
I don't believe I still care so maybe
I don't feel anything at all.

Because I don't care...
I don't.

I say this the whole walk to school.
Trying to convince the birds, the cars, and
the trees. Maybe even the sidewalk.
And especially
myself.

I Know No One Worth Knowing Here

and no one cares to know me.

It's the beginning of the year
and I'm sure this class is just as
pointless as I believed it would be.

The air in here
feels like dozens of dull pencils
pressed against my skin.

Everything about these walls
is too familiar. A cracked blackboard
and a white-faced clock with a black rim.
Loud creaking chairs that attach to
loud creaking desks.

Only 249 days to go and then ta-ta junior year.

Honeymoon Phase

Being with Nila is
different. Not because
she's a girl. (Though she is
the first girl I've ever been with.
The first anything, really).
It's different in a cheesy
movie kind of way. A
"spark" of sorts. When
she goes to hold my hand,
my heart doesn't stop. Doesn't skip
a beat or anything. But
wow, does it hurt.

Not the kind of hurt like when Mom died, though.
No, not that kind of hurt at all.

The First Time Nila Kissed Me

I was on my way out
from a party. We'd just met
that night. She walked me home
up to the front porch. When
she leaned into me, I asked her,
What kind of a girl wears cologne?

The kind who wants to, she replied.

Then she kissed my cheek and hopped
off the top step. *Night, Ginny*, she shouted.

I hate that name, I shouted back and went inside.

Fifth Period

I drag the
boulders that are my feet down
yellow-tiled halls.
When I arrive to my fifth class, I slop over
a front row desk like sludge.
I sit like I'm spineless.
My boneless body folds between
the desktop and the cold, green chair.
I jump when my back touches it.
Slam my knee against the desk.
Heads turn and look at me.

I hate this
place.

I wish
Nila was here.

Seating Chart

To my right sits
John.

He's gone to school with me
since I can remember. He hasn't changed
since then.

Story is,
his dad is a drunk and his mother's a ghost.
A living, breathing one, though.

Story is,
he has parents and I don't.

He's Been John

since I can remember.
Creepily quiet, but smart.
He wears the same three sweatpants every week.
And I can't remember the last time
I saw him out of a sweatshirt.
His round dimpled chin is
constantly tucked behind the collar.
It reminds me of the game Whac-A-Mole.
He takes his chin out to answer a question
in class, and then quickly tucks it back in.

Peppermint Patty

Gin stinks of
cigarette smoke. Bitter
and choking. The smell
makes my eyes water until
my nose is used to it. She wasn't
always a smoker. Gin
used to smell like peppermint.
Like the soft peppermints
that unfold and crumble when you
hold them in your cheek for just a few seconds.

My Place

I bring Nila here.
I skip my last period. Meet her outside school
just before football practice starts.
I take her hand. Guide her
into the forest behind the sports field. I have never taken
anyone here before
and I tell her this. She smiles and squeezes my hand.
Welcome to my place! I say.
And then we lay on a bed of red leaves.

Is this...

confusing? Nila asks. But
this is more than that. I remember
confusing. Confusing was the first time
I bled through my jeans. Confusing is
breaking down Shakespeare
for my AP English class.

This is not confusing.
This is that strange creep of déjà vu,
as familiar as a recent dream.
This is that rich, salty taste
of adrenaline after a race.
This is that warm prickle
of the sun on your skin
during a summertime rain shower.
This is the "A-ha!" moment.

This is...

home.

Nila Always Says Things

Spits "truths" she swears by—her
self-made bible.

Like she says it's better to "be out,"
to exist in the open.
She says this for the first time as
we lay beside each other on the grass.
Crossing pinkies.

When I imagine being free,
I imagine I'm a tree
and the sun is my truth,
bouncing warmth across my leaves.

The branches, my arms,
are wide and open.
I'm saying,
look at me, look at me.
I am free.

But we both know trees can't talk.

Nila Doesn't Say

how the choice of her story
wasn't really her choice at all.
At least not for a while.
That the "coming out" she speaks of
was more like she was thrown out.
And when I see
her as a tree,
I imagine her truth
like a forest fire.
Her leaves lit and burned.
Her fire spreading onto my branches.

When I Think About Truths

it makes me uneasy. Like church confessions.
I never quite understood confession. But I was too
afraid not to do it.

*Father, forgive me. I stole two dimes from Mommy's
dresser.*

> *Go and pray four Hail Mary's and help your
> mother with dinner.*

Even the smallest of things were
the biggest sins I had.

I Haven't Seen Nila

for nine days. I've kept track
with stonelike magnets on my
locker door. I slide a dark green one
beside the others to count 10. I
wonder if she's mad at me. If it has something
to do with my not being out. My phone
dings. She sends me a text. Wants to meet.

The Day Nila Dumps Me

I sneak out of school.
She dropped out a couple
of years ago. She often
asks me to skip, so
I do. When I meet up with her,
she's with her friends.
She says we are over. She says,
You bore me. Says this
in front of everyone.
We just don't mesh anymore, she says.
When I turn to leave, all eyes are on me.
Kids, man, I hear one person say.
In that moment, I feel like a kid.
I feel like a toddler.

I feel so small.

Bulimia Confessions

Sometimes, I want to confess to my mother.
I want to tell her the truth about this.
The dark, heavy *thing* in my chest that pulls
me to the toilet like a magnet. Pulls my fingers
to my throat like a forced habit.

Makes me throw up
every day
again and
again.

Pufferfish

I am taking off my backpack
when John turns his body to face me.
Why are your eyes so puffy? he asks.

Why are YOU so puffy? I snap back.

That was mean.

That was mean, I say out loud.

He mutters, *Yeah. It was.* Then he turns
to face the front of the class.
The starting bell rings.

Only 231 days.

She's Mean

and she smells even more
like cigarettes. Which
I didn't even know was possible.
She keeps coming in with red,
puffy eyes. They remind me of home.

At the end of almost every day,
my mother has those same eyes. Red
and puffy. Like she stuffed
them with cotton balls.
Like she filled them with helium.

The Afterlife

I feel as though I am
mourning a dead cat or my first goldfish.
Nila was my first goldfish. Bright orange
was her laughter. Her voice, smooth and velvet
 like waves. Fishy were her lips.
 She was my first goldfish. And rather
 than die, she leapt out of her bowl.
 Swam through my chest, passing
  my rib cage, out from between
        my shoulder blades,
         into bigger waters.

Fifth Period

When I walk into class
the next day, Gin is not there
and I am late. I am staring at her
empty chair when Mr. Ruzza slaps
a book onto my desk—*Romeo and Juliet*.
The loud slap of the book makes me
jump up, lifting the desk with me.
Someone snorts.
And then the whole class starts to laugh.

If Gin were here,
she wouldn't be one of them.
She never laughs
when the others do.

I Had to Get Out of There

I couldn't handle
the idea of class notes
or pop quizzes or gum popping.
The gossipy whispers or judgy glares.
So when I got to second period,
I walked right back out and went
to my place. But
it only reminded me of Nila.
And the way the red leaves
tangled in her hair
looked like the red freckles
that speckled her cheeks.
It was just too soon.

Uncle Leon

I just get home. And
Uncle Leon is standing with a paper in his hand.
A letter from the school about
my "lack of attendance." The first time they sent it,
I ripped it up. But they must've sent another.
He turns and faces me.
He looks so tired whenever he gets home
from his end-of-the-month business trips.
And when he is disappointed,
there is this look of betrayal
and a reminder of his trust in his eyes.
And I can't tell him how oddly
glad I am to see that face.
How it reminds me of Mom.

Home Sweet Home

Each day I open our front door
and I never know
what to expect. There are times
I find Father passed out in front of the TV.
There are times I find Father passed out
at the dining room table. Today,
he is standing in the kitchen archway.
And my mother is standing in front of him.
He's holding an ice pack in his hand. And
when he lifts it from my mother's face,
her eyes are red and puffy.
With purple rings to frame them.

Father

When I turned 10, my father
asked me, *Do you want to
be a man or do you want to be
a boy?* Confused by the question,
I didn't respond. He grabbed my
arms, shook me hard, and said,
No man calls his father "Daddy."
*You want to be a man? From
here on out, it is father or sir.
Do you understand?*
Yes, I said.
And then he squeezed
harder.
Yes, sir, I said.

Mom

pulled people in like a lasso. Drew
smiles out of faces that would rarely bend out from
their natural frowning form.
She was charming that way. Beautiful
and warm. Everything about her was fire.

Her dark brown eyes were like mine.
Her coily black hair was like mine.
Her laughter. Her voice.

Her exit, though,
was like Nila's—harsh, fast,
unexpected.

How She
Left Things

How Nila left me reminded me of Mom.
It was unexpected, unfair. It reminds me of a GIF I saw
that went viral across the school one day.
A toddler is on the beach by the
shoreline and a tall wave smashes into him.
Nothing bad happens, but when the tide pulls back,
the little one cries, sitting on the wet sand.

Everyone Laughed

when they saw the GIF. But I didn't.
I know how scary the wave must have been.
And when the toddler sits on the wet sand,
I imagine it is me. And it is quicksand
I'm sitting on. And I am stuck and sinking.

A Promise

I can still feel Mom's
hand wrapped around mine as
she walked me to my first day of school.
I made her promise she'd walk me every
first day after. I made her promise
she'd hold my hand right up to my classroom door.
Blue and red paper hand cutouts
all around its window frame.

When Mom Died

I begged her to take me
with her. I leaned over her casket,
took a hand that was
colder than ice. And I begged
that she walk me through my first
day without her. I begged her
to take me to the door where
"things get easier."

I begged her to take me.

Never

I was never warned
of all the ways
my heart could pump against
a surface other than
my rib cage.

Like, for instance,
the ground right outside
the door labeled
"first breakup."

Rather Than

Mom's hand to guide me
through it, maybe
brace me for what was behind
that door, for what happened
beyond its frame,
I felt
my body
thrown.
I felt
my body fall.
No hands
to catch me.
Not even my own.

Lately, When I See Gin

in the hall, I try smiling
at her. Because I figure if her
eyes are anything like my mother's,
then she must be sad about something.
Miserable, even.
And I'm not sure how to show her
kindness any other way.
But she hardly notices most people.
And if she doesn't notice them, she definitely
doesn't see me.

Crooked Smile

That kid, John, keeps
smiling at me in the hallways.
His two front teeth are crossed
like mine. And it makes me uncomfortable.
Each time, I look away. But it makes
no difference. He keeps smiling anyway.
So, today I stare.
I stare so hard that when his face
crumbles into sadness I almost
believe I broke it.

College Applications

I walk into
an ambush.
The guidance counselor
leans back in her chair.
She repeats the same question
she asked me last year:
What are your plans for college?
She hands me a pile of pamphlets
with strange faces.
Faces that look like
they know actual happiness. And
college is their source.

But the Smiles

look fake the longer
I look at them.
Their lips stretched so wide
I imagine them as a rubber band
that eventually snaps
from the tension.

When I Leave the Guidance Office

I look at my
reflection in the door window.
I try to remember what
that looks like across my face—a smile.

I wonder if it's even possible to do again.

Maybe somewhere fresh.

Somewhere new.

Maybe college?

Anywhere other than here.

College Plans

Nila would say
wasting money on college
is pointless. Because you could always
"self-educate." That never made much sense to me.
Because it was more than that.
My mom
would tell me stories of
meeting new people,
learning new facts,
making new things.
When I asked Nila if she thought these
stories were true,
she laughed in my face.

I Was Sure He Wouldn't Find Them,

but when I walk
into the house,
I find the papers spread out
across the dining
room table. A large brown bottle
is tipped over. Father
takes a college application—he
has been waiting for me
to see—and uses
it to soak up the spill.
His eyes are on me. A smirk slides
across his face.

Dinner

Father rants
about everywhere
I'm not going.
And everything I won't be.
My mother's lips part
and then quickly
press together around her fork.
I can't imagine what she would've said.
I can't imagine much of anything
in her voice anymore.

When Father

pierces the chicken
on his plate, I think
he imagines it's me.

He laughs,
mocking the applicant
requirements for an
Ivy League school.

He laughs so hard he chokes
on a piece of chicken.
And it's then that *I* imagine it's me,
stuck in his throat,
forcing him into silence.

When I Was Little

we'd gather around the TV
and watch *Jeopardy!* Father used to
throw popcorn in my mother's hair every
time she answered. Shushing her loudly through
her response. And when she got it right
(which really felt like always),
my mother's chin would tilt up. This is how
she'd show her closeted genius.
Quietly, and to herself.

Jeopardy!: Literature Edition

Shakespeare's tragedy Romeo and Juliet *was published in what year?* Mr. Ruzza asks.

What is 1597?
I say.

Correct, John, Mr. Ruzza says.
This was believed to be Shakespeare's first play.

What is King Henry VI?

Mr. Ruzza nods and claps,
which makes me smile.

Oh, we have ourselves a genius, Gin mocks.
She looks particularly miserable today.

A boy named Ricky laughs.
Then the rest of the class laughs.
But she doesn't.

She doesn't, but she made them.
And I don't know what
hurts most.

When I Was Little

my mother would shout from our house.
Come down, she'd say.
Come down from that wall.
The wall set the property line between the neighbors and us.
You can crack your head open
falling from up there, she'd yell.
I'd always burst into laughter,
knowing her head would poke out
once she saw me through the kitchen window.
And when I'd lose my footing, only then
would I get scared. Like Humpty Dumpty, I would crack.
Like an egg, I'd splatter.

Sometimes

I still walk to our old house.
I crawl
behind the hedges
growing below the wall
and I sit. I press against its
cool, gray-painted concrete
face. And I wonder: If I climb up,
will I hear her voice?

And then I remember
that if I fall, no one will be there
to help me.

For Sale

I was 13 when our house went up for sale.
It was cold and wet that night.
I left Uncle Leon's and found myself there.
If I throw a rock through the window, I thought,
maybe no one will want it.
So I did. I threw a rock through the front window.
And I ran
and slipped
and fell—
my jeans ripped through on both knees.
When I cried out, I wasn't sure
where the pain was coming from.

Sometimes

I get this itch
in the middle of my rib cage.
Maybe it's more like an ache.
And really it's always there.
Some days I think it's
just stronger than others.
It feels like the times you played outside
when you were little.
Your mother isn't there
and you fall.
Tears pool your eyes and
this pain grows in your chest.
Knowing you are alone. Knowing
you will have to pick yourself up.

Mr. Ruzza

asks John and I
to stay after class.
He lectures about how
I'm better than this. And
how John needs to stop
being late. He ends on a note
about finding friendship in loneliness
or misery or something like that.

I feel John look at me and
I want to apologize. Instead, I nod
and then I leave.

Today I Will Ignore Her

I'm not even sure
why I bothered
trying in the first place.
Mr. Ruzza is right,
misery needs company. But,
company and friendship
are two different things.

Gin isn't capable of either.

Today I Want to Be Better

so I try to catch John's eye
in the hallway. But
he never looks at me.
I realize for the first time
that we have the
same lunch period. But
he leaves through
the cafeteria doors the moment
he buys his food.

In class.
I'll just catch him in class.

He's Late When
He Finally Shows

So I don't get to say anything. But,
I notice a stain on the cuff of his sweatshirt.
It wasn't there when he walked out of the cafeteria.
I wonder what it's from. Then Mr. Ruzza
starts handing back our practice state exams.

Great.

I'll never get into college
at this rate.

Tutor Me,

Gin says. I don't respond.
So she says it again.
We got our test marks back
from our first practice exams.
Puh-leeeease, boy genius, she begs.
I laugh, but I'm not facing her when I do.
Out the side of my eye, I think
I catch her smiling. But I don't
turn to find out. I don't
want to risk it.

Lunch

Unlike me, when Johnny walks,
he shuffles fast. His legs are
like a hummingbird's wings.
I want to catch him. Maybe ask if he'd like
to sit with me. But today he's off again.
He has two trays in his hands, one flipped upside down
to hide what is on top of the other.
Quickly he is gone, like a rabbit,
through the double doors.
As if he is chasing something.
As if he has somewhere to be.

Broken Mirror on the Wall

who's the fattest of them all? *You are*,
it says. *You are*, again and again. My mother
insisted I try on these jeans for her. So I do.
And when I've had my fair share of the mirror's voice,
when I've seen enough
of my disgusting reflection, I crawl out of
the jeans. Slip into my sweats.

A Diet

I tried starving myself once.

I was 12 and in the
7th grade. I had gained some
weight. Sometimes in the
locker room, other boys would laugh
and point and poke at my stomach.

I didn't even make it a full two days before I
passed out in the middle of dodgeball.

Blue

From then on, my mother
would make sure I ate full meals.
TV dinners, snacks,
and cereal because
she worked double shifts
and was home only
a couple hours a day.

Like the blueberry girl in *Willy Wonka
and the Chocolate Factory*,
I watched
myself grow and grow.
And when they
started poking me again at school
and Father at home,

I'd sometimes pray
I'd pop
blue. All over the walls.
All over their faces.

Doubles

1.
I was about nine.
Father got let go
from his job. My mother sunk
all her worries deep in her belly.
When she first picked up
doubles at the diner, she'd drop me home
from school between shifts.
We'd sing songs the 20 minutes through.
Just to get us by, she'd say.
I'd nod my head in agreement.

2.

Months passed, turned into a year, and

Father was still home.

During those 20-minute drives, neither Mom nor I sung

anymore.

Just to get us by, she'd say when I'd get out of the car.

And they fought so much then, back and forth.

When she said this, all I heard was, *Just to get away.*

I'd bob my head in understanding.

3.
Father has a job now but isn't on strict hours.
He comes and goes when he pleases. But even
though my mother no longer
works doubles, she is even more absent now
than she was then. Every day feels like a trial.
And "just to get by," she doesn't fight back
anymore. She doesn't say or do anything all that much anymore.
I can't remember the last time either of us sang.

Tonight, I Wake Up

My mother
sits at the foot of my bed with
her hand on my ankle.
When I sit up, her eyes do not leave the floor.
I watch her lips part and
press back together.

She stands,
her head tilting slightly in my direction.
But she doesn't look at me before she leaves.

It feels like my lungs are swelling.
An ache grinds across my ribs.

I curl my head into my sheets.

If My Heart Had Knees

I wonder if she'd see they were bleeding.

Pools of blood and tears
filling the pit of my stomach.

I wonder how many bandages
it would take to close me up.

I wonder how much gauze.

John Wasn't Here Yesterday

He doesn't look at me
when he walks into class.

John looks tired.
More tired than usual.
And his skin—ghostly.
Mr. Ruzza puts a paper on my desk.

"Group Project: Scene Play"

And he assigns partners right
before the ending bell rings.
Before I can say anything
to John, he is out the door.

Romeo

was a fool. Like me, he fell for a girl
from a world he didn't belong to.
Like me, he chased with his heart first
and never thought about the risk.

Juliet

If my mother killed herself
for love, I wonder if Father would, too.
But, then again, my mother
already roams
like a ghost. Her body
an empty capsule.
Her chest a beatless, bruised tomb.

I'll Follow Him

That's what I decide to do—follow John.
So as he walks through the double doors, tray in hand,
so do I.
As he turns right, down Freshman Hall,
I do, too.
And when he walks up a ramp and turns left,
I also do this. I follow him
until he opens and shuts a door behind him,
a black and white PRIVATE sign stuck on its surface.

Thoughts from the PRIVATE Room

I try to remember the last time
I believed Father loved me. I try
to remember what he was like when he loved me.
Because I know that once upon a time
this time existed. But when I reach into my
mind, all I find is black, empty nothing.
As if I am no more than skin and bone.
No more than skin and skull.

Someone's Knocking

on my door.
This never happens. They knock again,
harder.
John? they say.

Oh god.

John? again. Is that Gin?

I crack the door and she presses an eye at the crack.

What are you doing here? I ask her.

What are YOU doing here? she asks back

as she tries to push through.

And I realize I haven't flushed the toilet.

The PRIVATE Room

I come here to eat my lunch
and throw it up.
A part of me wants to tell her this.
That two, sometimes three
fingers jam down my throat
three to five times a day.
Instead, I slam the door shut
on her fingers.

Nurse's Office

Gin is silent all the way there.
I keep a two-yard distance.
I watch blood drip down her right
arm. Nurse Kathy asks what happened.

Lockers?

And Gin looks up at me through the station window.
We hold this stare the whole time Gin
gets wrapped up.

Boyfriend? asks Nurse Kathy, when she sees
me out here
on the other side.
And then it's Gin who looks away.

It's Strange

I watch John stand there.
His face red with embarrassment.
Sweat beads on his forehead. I wonder
how he can feel so much worry, carry
so much sadness in his eyes.
His eyes don't look like everyone else's.
His sadness isn't generic
and fleeting. It's real. Like mine.

Real Sadness

When school started the year Mom died,
people talked about
the record-breaking heat.
But I don't remember if I
even saw the sun
that summer. If I felt its
warm rays across my face.

The night was my friend. The
night was quiet and the moon
was my sun. Cold and distant
like I wanted to be.

No one was around to say sorry for my loss.
I let no one in.
I knew their faces would hold frowns,
drooping like melted wax. Reeking of pity.
These faces brought me nightmares.

Mom's Voice

I couldn't find it anywhere.
It had once been so loud by that wall
when she was worried. I couldn't find
her face as lively in pictures as it
had been framed in our kitchen window.
I had to go back. I had to find her
in one of my most favorite forms.
Neck stretched over the window ledge,
head shaking. Voice cracking as it
found me.

And So One Night

I walked
to my old home to
sit between its hedges
and the garden wall.

See, the wall ran far down the
front lawn. I figured I'd never
be found there.
I figured I was safe this far away.
Even if a new family moved in.

The New Family

That night, the mother of this new
family went to let the dog out.
When she found him sniffing
near the end of the driveway,
she came to investigate. Once she saw
my face, she knelt down, cupped my
chin in her wrinkled hand. It had sun
spots like Mom's. And she
said, *Oh sweetie, I saw your*
face in the papers a little while back.
You come and go as long as you'd like.

I Had Refused

to come back for a few months.

I didn't need her pity, I thought.
I didn't need her telling me what I could
and could not do when this was my home once.

But eventually I did come back.
And no one ever came to chase me out.
She was generous.

She just let me be.

Generous

AP English
is not the only class John
and I will share now.
I find this out when the principal
calls me to his office the next day.
Mr. Collins has volunteered to shadow you.
He'll take notes for you until your hand
gets better. That's very generous of John.

Yes, I say and make sure he
sees my eyes roll. *Very generous.*

I Never Imagined Gin

to be the kind of person
to care for apologies. And
I figured if I was just a shadow
of a person any other day, she'd hardly
notice me following
her class to class. And I was right.
Because for a week she didn't
say a word to me. Well, until—

Why?

she asks. She stops walking.
Why was I there? I ask.
And when she doesn't
respond, I say,
Because it's my place.
My safe space. And—
She starts walking again.
She doesn't wait for
the rest. And I'm not
sure I would have
said much more anyway.

I'm Awake But It's 4 a.m.

I get up anyways.
Today, I shower.
I pull clothes over my skin.
I spoon cereal into my mouth.
I go to the bathroom.
I slide two bags of chips
between my lips.
I go to the bathroom.
I leave.

I Can't Sleep

School doesn't open for an hour. But I decide
today I'll just be early. I can't sleep knowing
that someone else knows about my safe space.
A room all to myself where no one can watch me.

Penmanship

Gin is reviewing our notes in
study hall.
You have really nice handwriting,
she says quietly.
Thanks, I say.
I feel like I should say something else.
You smell good today! I say.
She snorts.
You smell good today?
Ugh.
I quit smoking, she says,
and flips another page. *What
a weird compliment, by the way.*
So I try again.
You look nice in white, I say.
But it comes out so strange it
sounds almost like a question.
This time she goes cold.

White

I am a little girl.
My mother puts
white flowers in my hair.
She twirls me fast, faster,
(promises
hearts
of boys,
boys
that will make my head spin)
and then she stops.
The song comes to an end.
My flowers?
All over the kitchen floor.

When I Was
a Little Girl

my mother loved dressing me in white.
Every Sunday, she'd buckle me in.
Then, gently close the car door beside me.
I'd watch her white rosary sway
on the rearview mirror. Like a wind chime
in a summer breeze. The beads bouncing sun
rays like a disco ball.

I Saw a Woman Once

through the trees of the school forest.
Probably the mother of an away team's player.
Nervously watching, she brought her white
beaded necklace to her lips.

At night my mother,
rosary in her sun-freckled hands,
would kneel by her bedside and
bring her rosary to her lips.
Quiet whispers sweeping between them.

Sometimes I'd hear my name.

At Her Funeral

I heard people talking, whispering about how she
must've seen the other car coming.

That when they
pulled her from the car, her rosary was
in her hand. White beads scattered across the
dashboard. A few on the highway, rolling with the wind.

Love Me

I often wonder:
would Mom still love me
knowing I was gay? Or would she love me
knowing that it wouldn't be boys
that rushed blood to my face,
or made my head spin?

It wouldn't be a boy that caused
my second chest ache,
my second heartbreak.
Nila would always be my first.

I've Had This Nightmare Lately

Its meaning is all too clear.

I'm sitting on the couch in my uncle's house.

I can't remember who I'm speaking to. But they ask me,

What is it you wanted to tell me?

Well, I—and I start to choke. White beads falling from my mouth

into my cupped hands, onto my white, crisp-ironed skirt,

flooding the floor under my feet.

My Place with Gin

On the way to lunch, Gin asks me
about the room again.
So I take her with me. When I open my
door, she stands in the doorframe.
She looks at the toilet, the sink,
the chipped wooden bench.
Then she comes in. Closes the door behind her.
And sits legs crisscrossed
on the teal-tiled floor.

This First Time

we don't say anything and
I don't eat anything.

On Our Walk Home That Day

Gin trips and falls over a raised piece of sidewalk
and cuts open her knee.

I help her up.

On the Way Home

the other day, Johnny pointed out
how we both had our two front teeth
crossed, one over the other.
He made a joke saying we
must both be the mailman's kid.
But after he said this, and we looked at
each other, neither of us laughed.
In a way, we both wished it was true.

Gin and I

have been friends for
about 12 days. We haven't said
much on the subject, though.
Haven't used actual words about whether that's
what we're calling ourselves now.
Maybe I'm just her tutor still.
So maybe it's less than that for her.
Maybe it's eight…five…
or no days at all.

We Are Leaving School

and we see the USPS truck. Our mailman dad.
Both of us stop walking in our tracks.
And both of us try to hold in our laughter.
Afraid, I think, about how the other will react.
Until I see Gin's cheeks turn red and laughter bursts
out of the both of us in loud, ridiculous
cackles.

It's Strange,

but for seconds at a time,
every now and then
when we're together,
it feels as if maybe both of us are okay.
And at times even if we both seem
miserable, that is better than the
loneliness I felt before.

Before we were us.

We Talk

about our dreams, our hopes.
At least to some degree.
Johnny is vague. When we talk about what we
hope for in our future, when we finally leave this place,
I go on about the freedom we'll have. The ability to no longer
live like a herd animal, migrating only to the sound of bells.
Johnny says he hopes for "peace." But he never really says
much else.

Gin Always Changes Direction

when we get into a subject. She kind of
goes off track like a three-wheeled race car.
We talk about our lives after high school.
And as I say, "Peace," she comments on how strange
it is to be laying on a bathroom floor. And how strange it is
to be considered strange. And what necessarily is strange in the
first place? We never really go back to "hopes" after that.
Not really.

Johnny

and I have been friends
for four and a half weeks.
We are sitting in the PRIVATE room.
I tell him John
is a very serious name.
Well, I prefer Johnny, he says. I ask who
else calls him that.
No one but myself, he says.
I reach into his backpack
and doodle "ny's" whenever I
come across his name.

I think he almost cries.

Odes to Bulimia

1.
The first few times
we were (not friends but) familiar.
I had just turned 14 and
my father punched me in the stomach.
A Happy Birthday gift. Said it's not like
I could feel it anyway. With all that fat.

2.

After a few months,
it was safe to say we were friends.
Visits occurred nearly daily.
By then, I had new skills.
It took me less time.
It was almost easy.
It was almost
natural.

3.

Our anniversary is coming around.
But since Gin hangs around me more,
the PRIVATE room and I have grown to be bad friends.
I come here filled with both regret and
comfort. Both need and disappointment.
Like clockwork, the shifts come by
again and again. And I follow the routine
as best as I can.

4.

New schedule:

Once after breakfast.

(Sometimes) twice after lunch.

Twice after dinner.

Once before bed.

That way I can fit Gin in between.

And bulimia can stay

my little secret.

Can He Keep a Secret?

If I tell Johnny about Nila,
will he laugh in my face? Or
will he look at me disgusted?
If I tell Johnny, will he keep my secret?
Will he judge me? Will he
still be my friend? And how do I say it?
How do I bring it up? How do
I know?

Practice Makes Perfect

so I practice saying it out loud.
It's just me and trees. I say:
I think I'm gay.
I'm gay.
I like girls.
I like girls?
I change my tone, my posture, my volume.
Sometimes I stand. Sometimes I squat.
I even lay on the leaves, mostly because
my stomach is in knots. If I say it enough,
maybe it will feel natural to say to someone else.
Maybe it will feel natural enough to tell Johnny.

Empty

I come home
yet again to
an empty house.
It usually is.

When it is dark out,
I pack some snacks
in an old computer bag.
My mom once swore it belonged
to my father. I sling it over my shoulder
and walk back to my place.

Connect the Dots

I lay on my back in
the same spot I always do.
There is a permanent
grass angel in my shape.

I draw lines with my fingers
through the second
brightest stars. I name them
after Johnny. They're right
beside the brightest stars
I named after my mom.

Look Mom, I made a friend.

This Week

I have almost told Johnny
twice.

The first time was Monday
after we had
our Shakespeare
group presentations in
English. A group of all girls
recreated the "Secret Wedding" scene.
The one in Act 2 with the wedding of
Romeo and Juliet. There was even
a female friar.
I couldn't read Johnny's feelings
toward their version of
the scene. Sometimes I can't
read Johnny at all.

Some Boys

in the class whistled,
howled like dogs.
And it made my skin crawl.
It made my skin feel like red, raw meat
dangling in front of their snouts.

Ricky was one of them.
He yelped and cried,
"Mercy, ladies!" and the other boys laughed.
Like tumbleweeds, they rolled and turned in their seats.

Grade-A High School Romance

Ricky,

like Johnny,

is a kid I've gone to school with for years.

Ricky is the guy every girl

thinks she should have a crush on.

(I'm pretty sure I did freshman year.)

Just last week, I parted ways

with Johnny in the hall. Was

still laughing from what Johnny had said.

And then Ricky

passed me saying,

You look good when you smile.

And it doesn't

              make

                      sense.

Friday

Gin, Ricky says.

*Yes, Ricky? How may I
help you?* Gin answers
with sarcasm.

*I was wondering if you
would like to sit with me
at my table today*, he says.

Can Johnny come? she asks.

And we all know the whole cafeteria is watching.

Um, ha, well—

Then she cuts him off.

Thanks, Ricky, but
I'm going to have to say absolutely not.

And she shoulders past him to leave
through the double doors.

Freaks, Ricky mutters.

But you look so good when
you get rejected, Gin shouts on the way out.

Dear Ricky

The most unrealistic things to assume are:

1) That I would be flattered by you.
2) That I would want you to have any type of interest in me.
3) That I would have any interest in you.

But one thing's for sure, Ricky.

I am most
definitely,
totally
gay.

The Following Wednesday

I almost told Johnny.
We were in the PRIVATE room.
I have now named it "Cafeteria 2.0."
Hey, I'm not creative. Anyway, we always
eat lunch there. We had just come
up with our own friendship handshake. And
he said he
never had one before.
I almost told him then.

Thursday Night Dinner

I saw you met a girlfriend, my mother says.
I saw the both of you walking together.
She brings a forkful of food to her mouth.
And I don't get to think about
how she saw this because
Father begins to laugh. So hard tears come
to his eyes. *This ugly kid?* And he points
at me with his butter knife.
A girlfriend?

I think, what would
Gin say? Except I say
her response out loud: *Right.*
Because you look and smell
so much better.

Father flicks my bottom lip so quick, so hard,
it starts to bleed.
But I don't cry.

Lap Dummy

My poor mother
sits at the table. Her eyes down.
Both arms now dangle at her sides.
She reminds me of those puppets where
somebody's pulling the strings. One
made of wood. Not lifeless. But hoping
someone, anyone but him, would play
the master.

The Next Day

What happened to your lip? Gin asks.

I ran into a door, I say.

Seriously? she asks.

I fell down some stairs, I say.

Come on, she says.
She is frustrated now. We
arrive at our classroom.

I slipped in the shower, I say.

We take our seats
and her eyes roll.
The bell rings and Mr. Ruzza
begins the lesson.

My Lip Can't Heal

because every time I throw up,
the cut splits open again.
My mother doesn't know this.
Stop picking at the scab, she whispers.
She puts Neosporin on it
in my room. Then she bandages it
the best she can.
Brings me dinner in bed.

When He Hurts Me

Father usually
refuses to have
"family dinner"
for a couple
of days. It always makes
both my mother and I
breathe a little easier.

Lonely

I go another weekend alone
with my secrets. When it is dark,
I pack my bag and I head back out
to be with Mom. I lay out to look at
her stars.

*Would you still love me
like this?* I ask her over and over. Until
I am shouting.
I watch a large dark cloud roll over her.
Tears race down my face.
And then it starts to rain.
And all I can think is

she's crying with me.

I Love the Smell

of pouring rain. The way
some people love the smell
of fresh-cut grass. I love when it thunders.
When there are flashes of lightning. And
if you inhale deep enough,
you can taste copper.

My Birthday

will be here soon. And I
am already afraid. If I
could, I would fast forward.
Hit skip a dozen times. To
when I am in college and free.
I would run away if I could,
if I was strong enough to.

Like A Roller Coaster

Friday makes its way back around.
This week has flown by and I
haven't even thought about it. I'm
just not ready to tell my secret.
I just don't think I can tell him.
You can't practice for this.

Locker Talk

Ricky is leaning over my locker door
as I rush to switch textbooks for the long
weekend. The overpowering smell of his
body spray makes me want to throw up.
Gin, we had ourselves a cute little spat
the other day, he says. *Our first fight.* I slam my
locker door shut. Then start walking away.

Get a Grip

Wait, Gin, I thought
we could—

Everything
else Ricky says sounds
muffled. As if he is speaking through
a pillow. Because his hand
is on my shoulder now.
I feel my body forced
to spin and face him. I see
his face appearing larger
as it moves so quickly close to mine.
Then, I shove him. I push him so hard.
When his body
hits the lockers behind him,
I hear the textbooks inside
tumble like dominoes.

Dear Mom,

A boy just made
my head spin.
My body, too.
And I didn't
want him to.
I didn't like it.
So, I pushed him
and I ran.

Run

It all happened so fast.
Gin is running and I
run behind her. And
after a few turns I know exactly where
she is headed.
The closer we get to the
door, the louder
I can hear her sobs.
They echo in
my eardrums. They rattle
off the hall's walls.

Word Vomit

When I am safe in our PRIVATE room,
and my shakes calm down,
the truth just comes out of me.
So heavily, like
I suddenly have the flu.
I'm gay, Johnny, I say. And when he
doesn't say anything, I try again.
But it comes out softer, more afraid.
He just stares.

After a moment,
I can't stand the silence.
So I leave. I sprint down the halls.
Out the front doors. Straight through the trees.

I don't stop running until I am where I am supposed to be.
Lost.

Monday

Johnny didn't come to school today.

I told him
about me.

I told him and
he isn't at school today.

Tuesday

Like chalk, I am disappearing under the weight of an eraser.
The girls at school keep staring at me.
And the boys, too.
Their stares are different, though. Their eyes
are like fogged plastic. Uninviting and hard to read.
Did he tell
one of them?

No one is saying anything.
Not one thing.

Am I imagining the stares?
Am I imagining the whispers?

Wednesday.
Homeroom.

I hate him. I hope he got hit by a bus.

Fourth Period

I hope I get hit by a bus.

Sixth Period

I skip the rest of the day.

It is pouring. I am heading to my place. My place,
past the muddy baseball field. Through the tree line
that edges the baselines. I go and go until
I trip over a stump.
My hands are ready for the earth. My lip punches a low
branch. I stumble into a crouch,
then into a sit.
Until finally I am lying,
blood and rain running down
my chin.

I want to sink into soil.

I want to slip into sand like a snake.

I'm Not All That Familiar

with friendship. I
never felt a need to ask people
their secrets in exchange for my
own. Because no one ever really
found me worthy of their truths.
Of their fears. Of their time. Not
before Gin.

When she ran out the room,
a wave of guilt and joy washed
over me like a rain shower.
And she was gone before I
could open my mouth.

The Sunday

after Gin tells me her secret,
it's my birthday. I
spend the morning
in my room for as long as
I can. Then I hear my mother's
slippers shuffling. She
paces outside my bedroom door.
When I open my door, I
am afraid to pass through it. But
as I step out, I don't hear him.

He's not home.

A Cupcake

My mother lights
its red candle.
She looks so nervous,
I don't think she realizes
the candle is melting into the frosting.
Happy birthday, she whispers.
Her smile as full as a half-moon.
I blow out the flame and hug her.
The cupcake smashes
between her cupped hands.

I wished for her, then.

Three Blind Mice

Father comes home at noon with
three brown paper bags.
And a grin on his face so wide his
lips twitch. *One for you, one for me, and
one for good luck*, he says. He places
them on the table. *Come*, he calls,
waving his hand to sit down. But I wait.
Come, he says, louder now. A finger pointing down
to the seat beside him.

Today You Will Become a Man,

he says. And he pulls a bottle out, clear
as water. His large
clumsy hands
fumble with the seal.
When the cap is off, he grabs my right
wrist. He shoves the bottle into my
palm. *Take a whiff*, he says,
tilting it toward my face. I gag.

The Game

is simple, he says. *I sing*
you "Happy Birthday" and you drink
until the song is complete. Okay,
champ?

Thomas, please don't—
my mother starts.

Shut up, Father says between teeth.
On your mark...get set...cheers!

He clinks the bottles together.

I Am Choking

so he tilts the bottle up.
Happy Birthday to you! Happy Birthday
to you! And then he starts it back around again.
And when I vomit on the dining room table,
I feel a sting on the back of my neck.
Why'd you have to do that for?
You wasted it! We have to start again.
Mimi, grab a towel! he shouts. *Again, again!*
he says, a laugh between the words.
I can hardly see my mother's face.

When I Throw Up
for the Second Time

—or maybe it's my third?—
I see pink. Or is it red?
My stomach, I think I say.
My mother
—is she screaming or crying—
in the background?
You'll kill him, she says. *You'll kill him.*
And then I don't see anything at all.

She Is Standing In Front of Me

Nila
is standing in front of me.
I am sitting up from the fall.
And there she is—standing
in front of me. *Gin*,
she says, softer than cotton.
Am I chewing glass? I can't
speak. I tighten my jaw
to stop whatever jumble is
slipping between my lips. Then,
I bite down, harder. And
wet, salty iron coats my tongue.

Nila Says Something Else Now

She says so many somethings. And
I'm too confused to track the words. Until
she says, *Your friend. I think he's in the hospital.*

What? I ask.

Your friend, you know, my neighbor John?
I think he's in the hospital.

And I start sprinting. Through the tree lines. Tripping
on their roots. Through the muddy baseball field.
Past the school. Down the main city road.

.

The Hospital

I am screaming
in the front lobby for a boy named
Johnny. *Chubby kid, two crossed teeth
like mine.* I point at my mouth.
What room?! What room is he in?! Please!

The nurse just shakes her head.

Family only.

His Mother

is a small woman with pink eyes.
She takes my arm
and walks me to an elevator.
Then down a hall,
to a wide, half-curtained
window. This is where I see him.
Wires sticking out of his arms
like spider legs.

It's Immediate

The tears come first. And when I
see the half-inflated birthday
balloons by his bed, I lose
my head. I didn't even know
it was his birthday.
How did I not know? *I'm
so sorry. I'm so, so, so, so
sorry.* But I don't even know if
he hears me. I don't even know if
he cares.

All Eyes On Me

There are two pairs
of red puffy eyes when
I wake up. At first, I
wasn't sure if they were there.
But the harder I blinked,
the closer they became.
I watched my mother run out
into a bright hallway and
scream for someone. Someone
near me smelled just like peppermints.
But then I was asleep again.

This Time I Wake Up Nauseous

but I can't figure out where that's coming
from. When I finally
get my eyes to stay open, Gin is
asleep in a chair to my left. This
is the hospital. I am in the hospital.
My mother comes in from the direction
of a very bright hall. And she runs back out
again. *I need a nurse or a doctor please!*
she's shouting. *He's awake! He's awake!*

Visiting Hours

Hi, John. Good to see you awake, the doctor says.

Johnny! His name is Johnny, I say.
I can barely see his face with the doctor
standing in front of me, blocking my view.

We're going to try a few
tests real quick. Okay, John?
the doctor says.

His name is Johnny, I say again.

He's awake
and he's my
best friend.

A Best Friend

I never admitted it but I always
wanted a friend I could call my own.
We'd match bracelets. And finish
each other's sentences. And whatever
else best friends do in the movies.
What I didn't expect was to make a best
friend that didn't do any of those things.
Any of those things at all.

My Best Friend

is lying on a hospital bed.
And the only thing that matches
is our allergy bracelets. Because
I asked the nurse if I could get
one like his. *I'll tell everyone
we went to a really cool rave*, I whisper to
Johnny while he sleeps. And I laugh
because I know he would, too.

Me at a rave? he'd say.

My Best Friend Johnny

had a birthday I didn't
know about. Because I was too
caught up in my own misery.
My best friend was sick
and needed me. He's bulimic
and I was too busy worrying about
myself to notice. Maybe he was too busy
worrying about me, too.

When I See Gin

I tell her everything.
Everything I can remember.
And how there
are some things I can't.
I cry to her.
Tell her I'm sorry. Tell her
how I didn't mean to be so quiet that day.
How I wanted to say
the right thing.
And how I couldn't decide
if there was a right thing.
I tell her that I'm bulimic and beaten.
I tell her that I'm scared.

When I See Johnny

I tell him everything.
Everything I regret. And
how there are things I can't
regret.
I cry to him.
Tell him I'm sorry. Tell him
how I didn't mean to not pay attention.
Didn't mean to miss the red warning signs
on his strangely ghostly skin.
How I wished I was right there even though
I was there all along. I tell him
that I wish I told him I was gay sooner.
I tell him how I was scared.

Tug-of-War

We go back and forth. Like
tug-of-war with apologies.
Apologies that are so jumbled
with sobs that eventually we both
just stop. And then start laughing
so hard we cry again.

Look, I say as my mother pokes her head in
to check on us. *I made a best friend.*

Recovery

Johnny spends the next three weeks
in an eating disorder inpatient facility.
Not too far from home.
Every day after school, Mrs. Collins drives me there
and back in time for dinner. On weekends, I walk
early to her house, have breakfast, and then we
make our way to see Johnny again.

Mrs. Collins Cried

on my shoulder last night when I came over
for dinner. But before that she hadn't said much.
It was when I was leaving. Standing in her doorway.
She hugged me goodbye and then she cried.
I'm sorry, Gin, she said. Her voice breaking
somehow within those three words.

I Have Questions

and like most things I can't find
the right time to ask them. On this
Saturday morning, I feel anxious, unsteady,
as we drive to the treatment center.
Like a buoy in rapid waters.
Mrs. Collins, I say. But she doesn't respond at first.

I clear my throat.

Mrs. Collins, I try to say as
politely as the first time. But this time it
lands like a pinch. She jumps a little.

Hm? She Replies.

I inhale sharply and exhale it out.
What happened to Mr. Collins?
She says nothing and then we pull into a visitor's spot
and the gear is shifted to park. Then her voice is
suddenly so low, I hardly recognize it.
Jail, she says. *And I pray he rots.*

One of the Days

when Johnny is at the clinic, we make a pact.
It is simple. No more secrets.
And it reminds me of Nila and her Truths.
When I see myself as a tree now, there is a branch
that is fully bloomed. The other branches try but
need more light.

I Walk Gin Home

from school the first day I am back. She is holding
my hand. Sweat pools between our palms.
When she pushes her front door open,
her uncle is standing in the kitchen across from us.

Uncle Leon, she says.

I Push the Door Open

and Uncle Leon's standing in the kitchen.
He doesn't look up from his phone.
When I step back to abort the mission,
Johnny grips my hand tighter.
No more secrets.

Uncle Leon, I say.

Seuss

What's up, guys? Uncle Leon asks, still looking
at his phone. He's been back for eight days. I walk up
to the counter he leans on. Johnny is close behind.
It's so nice out, don't you think? I ask.
Uh-huh, he says.
And then it all falls out of my mouth at once:

I missed you, how was your day, also I'm gay, what do you say?

(I realize I sound like Dr. Seuss.)

Oh, he says, clicking off his phone. *Yeah, I know.*

He breaks into a smile. And when I exhale,
he stands beside me. Puts his arm
around my shoulder. Turns to look at Johnny and says,
Now what should we have for dinner?

Mr. Collins

There is no contact from Mr. Collins
after the arrest. We don't talk about him
because that's what we agreed on. After a
couple weeks of having Johnny home, I help
him and his mom unpack some boxes.
Fresh start, I say.

Mrs. Collins smiles and
says, *Oh, we're getting by.*

The Wall

At Johnny's new apartment,
there is a random wall.
We climb it sometimes.
When I climb up it today, Johnny
yells from below, *Mirror, mirror on this random wall,*
who's the greatest of them all?

You are, I say.
You are! he says back.

And as I bow
from up top, the old lady a couple doors
down shouts, *Get down from there! You'll crack your head open.*

And we laugh so hard as we run.
We laugh so hard
I think my face cracks.

Mother

She is humming now.
I can't really make out the song. I'm not
even sure it has any words.
But she's humming and it's beautiful.
So loud it fills every room of this
tiny apartment.

Every hall, every corner.

First Date

Gin has her first date today
since Nila. Her name is Julie.
They met when she
visited me at the treatment center
where Julie volunteers.

As Gin shifts her shirt,
she looks at me, tears forming in
her eyes.

Johnny, what if—

Knock 'em dead, killer, I say.

I squeeze her really tight.

Break her heart, I say.

But I know
that Gin is not the kind
to break hearts.

First Date Questions

Your first celebrity girl crush? I ask.
Easy, Julia says. *1990s Julia Roberts!*
I laugh. *That's cute*, I kid.
Julie and Julia sittin' in a tree!
She tickles the palm of my hand
that she's been holding.
And you? she asks.
I take a large bite of my slice of pizza
to stall time. *Jolie*, I say,
my cheeks now full of crust.
What?
Angelina Jolie! I shout
in the middle of the food court.
And we both almost
fall out of our chairs,
we laugh so hard.
Soda dribbles out her nose,
we laugh so hard.

This Summer

goes by fast, even though
I am taking it slow. We spend
most of our days sitting on the wall.
It's wide enough that we can play
board games and cards on top.
And if we aren't there, we are inside.
Having dinner with my mother or
at Gin's house, playing catch in
her small backyard. Recovery
feels so far away, college even farther.
So we measure our days in small parts.
We take our time, for both of our sakes.
Not as much hers, it seems, as mine.

Senior Year

I am back here again
and not much is different.
The clocks still have black rims.
Classrooms still smell stale.
All the chairs are still that ugly green.
The halls still have
gritty yellow tiles.
But
this year is our final year.
And this time I've got
my best friend.

Here Again

Finding myself here again
feels like throwing a found
needle into a larger haystack.

Four Weeks Later

I haven't run
into Johnny so far today.
But, I don't think
much of it.
Our classes don't line up as well
as they did last year.

I tell myself
it's because of this.

It Has Been a While

Maybe a couple of weeks since I last had
dinner at Johnny's. Tonight, I'm back.
Heading back from the bathroom,
I catch Johnny in his room pinching his skin
and poking himself in the stomach. He is standing
in front of his bedroom mirror.

Broken mirror
on the wall, he says. *Who's the—*

Fairest, I interrupt. *Fairest of them all. Johnny, you*
are. You're the best.

When he sees me, he slowly folds toward the ground.
I kneel with him and catch his head with my lap.
His tears darken my jeans.

Mirror Image

When I look at Johnny,
it's like standing in front
of my reflection.
There are layers, mixtures
of joy, fear,
and misery in him.
And they mirror
mine. And I think how
I have never found
that in anyone else.

Guidance

I have another meeting with
the guidance counselor today.
For once, I'm not dreading it.
A corner-torn
paper is clipped to tomorrow's
history assignment.
It has a list of colleges
I've sent an application to.
For once,
my future seems
bright.

But

when I get to guidance,
I don't see pamphlets
spread out like a fan
on the desk. Instead
I see the counselor's hand stretched
out, asking me to take a seat.

It's About Johnny

She keeps talking, but I can't hear.
All I can see is her hand.
All I can think is how red her nail polish is.
Blood red, I think, red as the blood
that rushes to my ears.
My cheeks.
I don't need to hear her, though.
I already know what has happened.

Johnny Relapsed

He has made visits to the PRIVATE room
without me a couple of times this week.
He admits he did it again and again
the four weeks before.

Routine

Mrs. Collins and I start up
breakfasts again. I visit Johnny almost
every day after school. And like before,
she remembers to avoid
the highways because of Mom.

At times, even Julie comes
along to "hitch a ride to volunteering,"
but really to lend a hand.

I Don't Talk to Johnny

about how well things are going between Julie and I.
I don't talk about what he missed at school.
No, not this time around.
When he wants silence, I'm quiet.
When he wants to play board games, we play them.
When he needs to cry, we cry together.
And sometimes he refuses our visits.

This time around is different.
This time around he feels defeat.
It has swallowed him whole.

Second Try

When Johnny comes home, he is struggling
more than the first time. I come over
after school for dinner and tutoring some days.
Remind Johnny that he is the smartest of
us two. I hug him tight before I leave.
And sometimes, he doesn't hug back.
His arms underneath my squeeze feel weak. His bones
feel as if they bend to my grip. As if they could snap.

In My Dreams

Johnny is a small bird.
I go to reach into
his cage and tape up his wing.
But when I try, he's just
too far out of reach. It's almost
like he's afraid.

Or am I?

I Don't Talk to Johnny

about how Julie and I broke up.
How much it hurt. I don't talk
to Johnny about
such things because
he's my best friend
and I want to spare him
my sadness since
I can't spare him his own.

Five Weeks Later

With counseling, my lungs
feel as if they are able to expand
a little easier as time goes by. Sometimes,
the fear of relapsing feels as if one of my lungs
has cracked.

But jeez, does it feel good to breathe.

My First Letter

Mrs. Collins has us over for dinner,
Uncle Leon and me. I haven't opened it yet.
Johnny insists that any college letter
"calls for celebration regardless of the answer."
I slide the small envelope across the table.

I Pick It Up

and even though
it's light, both Gin and I have
held it like it's lead.
Every move I make opening
it is fast. I know she is impatient.

When I see the first few words,
I begin to cry.

Johnny's Crying,

so of course I cry, too. And I don't
even know what the letter says.
You've been accepted, he screams.
Somehow sobbing while smiling.
I've been accepted, I scream,
and I do the same,
a crash of emotions.
Uncle Leon and Mrs. Collins just grin
at us.

For Now, We Are Okay

Gin's acceptance letter helped me
realize a few things.

1. "All college acceptance letters come in
a big envelope" is a myth!

2. It's okay that sometimes
where you saw yourself,
who you saw yourself with,
or what you thought you never could do,
all change.

3. Just because you're walking
at your own pace
doesn't mean you're moving slow.
It just means you're taking
your time.

That time is yours.

When I'm Ready

I will send in my applications.
But like our
summer, I find myself wanting to meet
smaller goals still.
Between counseling, the rest
of senior year, and graduation,
I choose not to add anything else to my plate.

When I tell her all of this,
my mother grabs my arm and
with a smile on her face she squeezes it
tight.

From now on, it's not just to get by.
It's to get through, she says. And just
like the times when I was little, when we'd
sing in the car between school and double shifts,
it feels like we are in this together.

And it feels like peace.

Supernova

If anyone ever asks what
I'd like to be in the next life,
I'll say a star. Because they're Gin's
favorite. And because I imagine,
like the nova of streetlights,
how wonderful it must be
to bounce and shine
on the leaves of trees.

The Brightest Stars

We lay on our backs. Johnny points at
three of the brightest stars. And he says,
Look Gin. It's you. Not knowing that
those three make up a part of Mom.

I put my hands behind my head.
Yeah, Johnny, I say. *I can see that.*

WANT TO KEEP READING?

If you liked this book, check out another book
from West 44 Books:

A PERFECT BLANK
BY RYE DURAN

ISBN: 9781538382851

A Blank Beginning

I remember the day
I was born.

This is important
because I was not born
the way other
babies are born.
And I was not born
to be like
other babies.

The room was so
bright. There were
nine others. Exactly nine
others born that day. Nine
like me. None like me.

A speaker boomed
over each of us.

From my speaker
came a voice.
And that voice
said *Alex, Alex, Alex, Alex, Alex, Alex.*

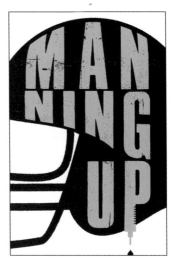

Check out more books at:
www.west44books.com

An imprint of Enslow Publishing

WEST **44** BOOKS™

ABOUT THE AUTHOR

Raised by her Haitian grandmother, Rayel Louis-Charles is a multiracial, queer author who identifies as, first and foremost, a poet. She has participated in spoken word competitions and drama performances. Much of her writing is a result of her personal traumas and struggles with identity and abandonment, as well as her own discoveries, hopes, and accomplishments. She hopes to reach young teens with her novel in order to remind a lonely young heart that this loneliness exists in others as well. Also, to stress the importance of consideration for others, not knowing that their story could be similar to your own.